Piles of Pets

By Judy Delton

Illustrated by Alan Tiegreen

A Stepping Stone Book™

RANDOM HOUSE 🏠 NEW YORK

For Craig,
the newest member of the family.
—J.D.

Text copyright © 1993 by Judy Delton
Illustrations copyright © 1993 by Alan Tiegreen
Cover illustration copyright © 2009 by David Harrington

Originally published by Yearling, an imprint of Random House Children's Books, a division of Random House, Inc., in 1993.

Random House and the colophon are registered trademarks and A Stepping Stone Book and the colophon are trademarks of Random House, Inc.

Visit us on the Web! www.steppingstonesbooks.com
www.randomhouse.com/kids

Educators and librarians, for a variety of teaching tools, visit us at
www.randomhouse.com/teachers

Library of Congress Cataloging-in-Publication Data
Delton, Judy.
Piles of pets / by Judy Delton ; illustrated by Alan Tiegreen.
    p. cm. — "A Stepping Stone Book."
Summary: To earn a badge during "Be Kind to Animals Week," Molly opens her house to a variety of needy creatures, but must then ask the Pee Wee Scouts to help her find permanent homes for her temporary pets.
ISBN 978-0-440-40792-8
[1. Pets—Fiction. 2. Scouting (Youth activity)—Fiction.] I. Tiegreen, Alan, ill.
II. Title.
PZ7.D388Pil 2009   [E]—dc22   2008043608

Printed in the United States of America   27 26 25 24 23 22 21 20 19 18

Contents

Good Deeds All Around

BE KIND TO ANIMALS WEEK, said the poster on the tree in the park.

Underneath those words were smaller words.

Adopt a Pet, it read. *Give a Home to a Four-Legged Friend.*

There was a picture of a big shaggy dog face with sad eyes on the poster.

"We have a pet already," said Mary Beth Kelly. "We have two. A dog and a cat."

1

"Mrs. Peters has Lucky and Tiny," said Molly Duff. Mrs. Peters was the Pee Wee Scout leader of Troop 23.

"I'm allergic to pets," said Tracy Barnes. She sneezed. "See, I sneeze if I even look at a picture of a dog."

"That's silly," said Lisa Ronning.

"No, it isn't," said Rachel Meyers. "It's psychological."

No one in the Pee Wees knew such big words as Rachel.

"You mean it's all in her head," shouted Roger White. "Ha, Barnes, it's all in your head!"

Tracy gave Roger a punch on the shoulder.

"Ow, ow, ow!" shouted Roger, pretending the punch had hurt. "Oh, my poor arm!" He fell to the ground and pretended to be wounded.

Tracy gave him a kick. "It's not in my head." Then she sneezed again.

"My mom won't let me have a pet," said Rachel. "She said animals have germs and they shed hair all over the furniture."

"A dog is man's best friend," said Sonny Stone. "What does a little hair matter?"

Rachel shuddered. "Well, I don't like to eat dog and cat hair in my cereal, thank you."

Molly wished she had a pet. She didn't have any brothers or sisters. It was the least her parents could do, she thought. They could buy her a pet to keep her company. A pet to stroke and cuddle and feed and love and take for a walk. Maybe Be Kind to Animals Week was the time to ask for one.

The Pee Wees were on their way to their Scout meeting. When they got there,

Mrs. Peters was waiting for them. She had a big smile on her face. Her baby, Nick, was smiling too.

The Pee Wees sang their song and said their pledge.

Then they told the good deeds they had done during the week.

Everyone wanted to be first.

"Mrs. Peters, I shared my ice cream cone with a stranger," said Tim Noon.

"You aren't supposed to talk to strangers," muttered Lisa.

"I didn't talk to him," said Tim.

"Hey, how can you share an ice cream cone?" shouted Roger. "You can't cut it in half!"

"I'll bet he gave someone a lick," said Mary Beth.

Mrs. Peters looked as if she did not know whether Tim's good deed was a good deed or not.

"He was my brother's friend," said Tim.

"Then he wasn't a stranger," said Roger.

"I never met him before," said Tim.

Roger hit his forehead with his fist.

"And I ate half of the cone and gave the rest to George. That's his name."

"Good for you, Tim," said Mrs. Peters, relieved.

Hands were waving.

"I passed out ads for Congressman Kent," said Kevin Moe. "I put one in every mailbox on our block."

Kevin liked politics. He wanted to be mayor someday. Molly liked Kevin. She secretly wanted to marry him when she grew up.

"We had the mayor over to dinner last week," said Rachel.

"Hey, that's no good deed," said Roger.

"It is too," said Rachel. "It's good to give someone dinner, isn't it, Mrs. Peters?"

"Well, it isn't bad," said their leader.

"She just wants to brag about how her dad is a friend of the mayor," whispered Mary Beth to Molly. "She wants to be a bigger politician than Kevin."

"I changed a lightbulb for my grandma," said Kenny Baker.

"I threw the old one away," said Patty Baker, Kenny's twin sister.

"Hey, how many cowboys does it take to change a lightbulb?" asked Roger.

Mrs. Peters frowned. "Let's talk about good deeds," she said.

"I helped my dad park the car," said Molly when she was called on.

"Hey, you can't drive!" shouted Sonny. "How could you help park the car?"

"Crash, bang, whang!" said Roger, with his hands on an imaginary steering

wheel. Soon more of the boys were careening around the room, parking imaginary cars.

"Eeeeek, boing!" squealed Tim, pretending to park between two chairs.

"I didn't drive the car," said Molly when Mrs. Peters had quieted the room down. "I got out of the car and saved the place till my dad backed the car in. And he didn't crash."

"Good for you, Molly," said Mrs. Peters. "Now we are ready to discuss something new."

The Pee Wees sat up straight. They wanted to hear about something new. Something new that they could get a badge for was the second most fun thing about Pee Wee Scouts. The first most fun was Mrs. Peters's cupcakes.

"Is it a treasure hunt?" asked Rachel.

"We had a treasure hunt at my cousin's birthday party."

"Is it a party?" asked Tracy.

"A contest?" asked Kevin.

Mrs. Peters held up her hand for silence.

"It's none of those things." She laughed. "If you don't keep quiet, I can't tell you what it is!"

The Pee Wees kept quiet. They turned a make-believe key in their lips, and threw it away.

"What is new," said their leader, "is Be Kind to Animals Week."

"Pooh," said Sonny. "That's not new. There are posters all over the place about Animals Week."

Now everyone began to talk about the pets they had or used to have or were going to have, and Mrs. Peters had to hold her hand up again.

"The thing that's new," Mrs. Peters went on, frowning at Sonny, "is that Troop 23 is going to do something special for Animals Week."

"I can't adopt a pet, Mrs. Peters," said Tracy. "I'm allergic."

"My mom says pets shed and have germs," said Rachel.

"We don't have to adopt a pet," said their leader. "We already have a mascot."

"Arf arf arf!" barked Lucky when he heard Mrs. Peters say "mascot." He knew he was the mascot. He had been the mascot of the troop for a long time.

"What I thought we could do for Animals Week," she went on, "is learn how we can be kind to animals. Learn tips to make them happy. Find some good deeds we can do for them. If you know of a stray animal, find it a home. Offer to take a pet for a walk. Baby-sit a pet for an owner over a weekend. Maybe we could even start a pet club. Those with pets could meet and let their pets play together. You could make an animal toy, or grow some catnip in your garden, or make posters about being kind to animals. We might even have a pet race.

"At the end of Animals Week, we will give out badges to everyone who has helped a pet in some way."

"Yay!" cheered the Pee Wees. They loved badges.

"I think pets would fight in a pet club," said Lisa. "I know my bird wouldn't like to come to a club that had cats in it."

"He could be in a cage, silly," said Roger. "Anyway, Tweetie Pie always gets away from Sylvester."

Roger the Cat went diving after Sonny the Bird, who scrambled under the table where the Pee Wees were sitting, bumping into legs and knocking over chairs.

Mrs. Peters clapped her hands.

"We will work out all of those details later," she said. "I just want you to be thinking about how Be Kind to Animals Week can apply to you. Now we will have our refreshments."

Mrs. Stone, Sonny's mother, came down the steps with the cupcakes and milk. She was the assistant troop leader.

After they had eaten, the Pee Wees drew pictures of pets. Molly drew a dog because that was the pet she wanted to have. Then they played games in the backyard, and sang their song again. It was time to go home.

At the corner was another poster of the dog with sad eyes. When they got there, Roger got out his black crayon from his backpack and drew a mustache on the dog. Then he drew a pipe in the dog's mouth, with smoke coming out of it. Last

of all, he drew eyeglasses on the dog's eyes that hooked over his shaggy ears.

"Roger White, you are defacing public property!" shouted Molly. "You erase that this minute."

Molly got out her eraser. But it didn't work. The crayon just smeared and made the picture worse.

Roger roared with laughter.

"Pet abuse! Pet abuse!" shouted Lisa.

"It is not. I'm not hurting that dog!" cried Roger. "He doesn't feel a thing!"

"Rat's knees!" said Molly.

"Roger only does that stuff for attention," said Mary Beth. "Just ignore it and walk away."

But when the Pee Wees left, Molly looked over her shoulder and noticed that Roger was drawing a red hat on the dog's head.

"We should tell Mrs. Peters," said Molly.

But she knew that wouldn't stop Roger. Roger was mean. And Mary Beth was right. He liked attention. And he would do anything to get it. Well, almost anything, thought Molly.

CHAPTER 2

Pet Talk

At suppertime Mr. Duff said, "What was new at Pee Wee Scouts today? What badge do you earn next?"

He passed Molly the pasta with seafood.

"Be Kind to Animals Week is coming up," said Molly. "And I have no pet."

"Do you have to have a pet to get a badge?" asked Mrs. Duff.

Molly wished she could lie. Here was

her chance. If she said yes, her mother might get her a pet of her own! If she told the truth, she would have to admit that Mrs. Peters had not said they must have a pet to get a badge.

Molly shook her head. She could never lie to her own mother. Or father.

"But we have to do something nice for an animal, and it would be easier if I had one of my own. If we adopt one, we can get our badge just like that. Just for taking him out of the pound."

"How about a goldfish?" said Mr. Duff.

Molly stared at her father. A goldfish was pretty, but surely not a good pet. It couldn't do a thing but swim. And eat. You couldn't hold it or cuddle it or take it for a walk or buy it toys.

"Then if you got tired of it, we could

pop it in our pasta and have it for supper!" he said.

Now even Mrs. Duff looked shocked.

"Daddy!" said Molly. "You could never eat a pet!"

Even if the pet was a fish with no personality, thought Molly.

"I should hope not!" said Mrs. Duff, pushing her seafood to the side of her plate.

Mr. Duff cheerfully took seconds.

"I'd like a dog of my own," said Molly wistfully.

"You can visit Lucky anytime you want," said her mother.

"It's not the same as my own," said Molly. "It's lonely without any brothers and sisters. A pet would help."

A tear rolled down her cheek. Now Molly felt guilty. This was corny, she could see that herself. Trying to trick her parents into getting her own way!

"You have me!" said her father. "Arf! Arf! I can play ball with you and sit up."

"A pet is a problem when we want to go out of town to Grandma's," said Mrs. Duff. "Or on a vacation. And they need to be walked and groomed and go to the vet for shots. Now that I'm working part-time, we can't do all those extra things."

Molly's mom had a part-time job at Ace Insurance Company.

"Maybe a small pet," said her dad. "A turtle or a snail that could take care of itself."

Molly would rather have no pet than have a turtle or a snail! All the kids who couldn't have a real pet got those. The kids who were allergic, or had babies in the family, or whose mothers hated fur and germs.

"Could you rent a pet?" asked Mr. Duff. "You know, keep it till you have your badge, and then take it back?"

"You mean I can have a pet for a little while?" said Molly.

Her mother looked at her father.

"Well, temporarily, I suppose," said her mother.

"Like a guest," said her dad. "It could visit and then go home."

Having a guest pet sounded interesting. If she couldn't have a permanent pet, a guest might be the next best thing. It gave Molly an idea.

The next morning on the way to school, Mary Beth said, "What are you going to do to get your badge?"

"I'm going to take in homeless animals," said Molly. "I'm going to cheer them up and then I'll find them a home."

"Really?" said Mary Beth. "Boy, that's

a real good thing to do for Animals Week! Will your mom let you?"

Molly nodded. "She said temporary was okay."

Her mother hadn't said how many temporary pets she could have. But she hadn't said "You can only have one pet" either. She must have meant as many as Molly wanted as long as they would not stay forever.

"All I can think of is taking pets for a walk," said Mary Beth. "Like Mrs. Graf's old Shep."

Shep was old, thought Molly. But not as old as Mrs. Graf. She could use some help walking him.

"That's a good idea," said Molly warmly.

"But not as good as yours," said Mary Beth.

She was right. It would be more fun to

have a home for homeless animals than it would be to walk Shep.

When they got to school, all the Pee Wee Scouts were talking about what they wanted to do for Be Kind to Animals Week.

"I'm going to donate my services to the local pound," said Rachel. "I can brush the cats or something."

"My dad said I could adopt a pet," said Roger. "Maybe I'll get a lion or a tiger."

"Ha ha ha," said Sonny. "Those aren't pets. Those are zoo animals."

"Well, I'm getting a rare animal," said Roger. "I don't want any old dog or cat like everyone else."

"I'm getting a more rarer animal," said Sonny. "Something you won't ever get. I might adopt a leopard."

"Sure, Stone," said Roger. "And he'd leap up on your bed at night and eat you!"

"So would a tiger or a lion!" shouted Sonny. "You think you're so smart!"

All week the Pee Wees thought about how to get their pet badge. They thought about what good deeds they could do for a pet. And Molly kept her eyes open for strays without homes.

At the next Pee Wee meeting, Mrs. Peters listened to ideas.

"I think Molly's idea is wonderful!" she said. "Just be sure you can carry out your good deed. Think about it before you begin. Molly must be sure she can find homes for the animals she takes in, in order to get her badge. Those who adopt a pet must be sure to give it a good home and care for it. Feed it, exercise it every day."

Molly was sure she could find a home for a pet. Everyone wanted a pet. Pets were fun to have. And hers would be free. They would not cost money like in a pet store.

"I'm going to choose something easy," said Lisa. "Like growing catnip and selling it."

Mrs. Peters clapped her hands. Everyone stopped talking.

"I have a little surprise today, boys and girls. We have a guest from the animal pound to speak to us. He is an animal expert, and can give us lots of tips on animal care, and tell us some things we don't know about animals."

A man came down Mrs. Peters's steps. He was tall. He was smiling.

But the thing the Pee Wees saw first was what he had on his shoulder. It was a bright red-and-green-and-blue parrot. The parrot had a sort of leash attached to his foot. The other end was in the man's hand.

"Oh, I want one!" shouted Sonny. "I want a parrot!"

Everyone laughed.

"Of course he'd want one," said Mary Beth to Molly in disgust. "He wants everything. He's such a baby."

"I'd like to have one too," said Molly. "They talk."

"This is Mr. Sharp," said Mrs. Peters. "And his parrot, Sunny."

Now everyone roared. They looked at Sonny and pointed. "You've got a parrot's name!" yelled Roger.

"This bird's name is spelled S-u-n-n-y," said the expert. "Because he's so happy."

But the damage was done. "Parrot Face, Parrot Face," Roger yelled, pointing at Sonny.

"Most birds like Sunny belong in the wild and should not be bought as pets. But Sunny was raised by humans since he was hatched. His wing is damaged, so we can't release him back into the forest," said Mr. Sharp.

He told the boys and girls all about Sunny. What he ate. Where his wild relatives lived. And how his wings worked.

"Most parrots are called Polly," said Rachel out loud. "Just like Molly, only with a *P*."

Wasn't it enough that the bird had Sonny's name? thought Molly. Did Rachel have to drag in other names he *could* have had?

"Most birds like seeds," said Mr. Sharp. "And some vegetables like grated carrot. If you have a pet bird of any kind, or are putting out food for wild birds, don't feed them peanut butter. They like the taste, but it makes their bills stick together. If their bills stick shut, they can't eat. And then they can starve."

Molly wrote that down in her pet notebook. *Never give a bird peanut butter,* she wrote.

Sunny fluffed out his beautiful feathers while Mr. Sharp spoke. Every once in a while the parrot said, "Sunny is a good bird."

The Pee Wees clapped when he did that.

After Mr. Sharp spoke about grooming birds, he spoke about grooming dogs and cats. He used Lucky to demonstrate.

"Always brush an animal's fur in the direction it grows," he said. "Not backward."

Lucky seemed to enjoy being brushed.

"Here are some other tips," he said.

Molly got out her notebook again.

"Never yell around animals," he went on. "It frightens them, and it hurts their sensitive ears."

"All pets like fresh, clean water," said Mr. Sharp. "If you have a pet, be sure to change the water in his or her dish often."

"We give our cat fresh milk," said Mary Beth.

"Water is better for them than any other drink," said Mr. Sharp. "Even better than milk, which can make adult cats sick.

"And while we are on that subject, bones are dangerous for dogs. Almost all bones. There are toys for pets to chew that will not splinter or hurt their teeth. But bones are dangerous."

"Dogs like bones," said Roger in disgust.

Mrs. Peters frowned at him.

"It's just like Roger to know more than an expert," whispered Tracy.

"Remember," said Mr. Sharp, "if you take your animal in the car in summer, always leave the windows open if you leave it alone. Pets can die from being locked in a hot car in warm weather."

When Mr. Sharp was through talking,

the Pee Wees filed past Sunny to get a good look at him. Roger gave him a pat on the head and Sunny gave him a peck on the hand.

"Hey, that bird bit me!" shouted Roger, rubbing his hand.

31

"He didn't bite anyone else," said Rachel to Roger. "He doesn't like you."

Mrs. Peters thanked Mr. Sharp for coming. So did the Pee Wees. He said good-bye and so did Sunny.

"Bye-bye," said Sunny, all the way up the steps and out the door.

Mrs. Peters went over the things Mr. Sharp had said. All the Pee Wees wished they had a parrot. But Molly had other things to think about. She had her home for pets on her mind.

CHAPTER 3

Homeless Pet Home

That afternoon after the meeting, Molly went home and made some signs.

"Can I put your phone number on my signs?" Molly asked Mary Beth over the telephone.

"Why?" asked Mary Beth.

"My mom might be at work," said Molly.

"Okay," said Mary Beth. "I'll take their numbers and you can call them back."

It was true Molly's mother and father were both at work. Some of the time. But if Molly was to admit the real reason for using Mary Beth's phone number, it was that she was a little bit afraid of what her mother might say about the home for homeless pets. Even if it was temporary.

Molly made five signs. They said, WANTED: HOMELESS ANIMALS. CALL 555-4608. She drew a picture of a lost animal on each one. Then she went out and hung one on a tree in the park and one on the bulletin board in the grocery store.

The next day at school she hung a sign on the bulletin board in the hall where all the lost-and-found notices were. She needed two more places.

"How about the drugstore?" said Mary Beth. "There is a billboard out in front."

Molly ran there at lunchtime. When she passed a church, she noticed a board there. One notice said, SAVE SOULS. Well, that was surely what Molly wanted to do. The souls of lots of poor pets. She hung her last sign at the church and went home to wait, and to plan where she was going to put her guests. She might have to hide some of them just in case. In case her mother or father misunderstood. But who could complain about doing a good deed? About getting a badge for Pee Wee Scouts? Mrs. Peters herself had said Molly's idea was a wonderful one.

But Mrs. Peters's other words kept coming back to her. "Molly must be sure she can find homes for the animals she takes in, in order to get her badge."

Well, Molly surely could do that. She would take the pets in and give them out. All as quick as one, two, three.

On Saturday Mrs. Peters called a special meeting of the Pee Wees.

"I had some ideas for Animals Week," she said. "I thought it would be a good idea to keep scrapbooks of rare and unusual pets. You can watch for pictures in magazines and bring them to our meetings and we will put them all in one big scrapbook."

The Pee Wees cheered. They liked to collect things.

"And since so many of you have pets, or are adopting pets, I thought we could have a pet race next Tuesday, just for fun."

"Yeah!" shouted the Pee Wees. They loved races too.

"Then we can talk about what you are doing to help pets and earn your badge."

The Scouts helped Mr. Peters give Lucky and Tiny a bath. They scrubbed them down with antiflea soap. Then they rinsed the dogs with the hose. Before the

Pee Wees could jump out of the way, Lucky and Tiny shook themselves. Water went everywhere. Onto Mr. Peters. And Mrs. Peters. And all the Pee Wees.

Roger held his nose. "Wet dog," he said.

"It smells good," said Molly. Molly liked everything about dogs. Even the smell of wet ones.

"Hey, what kind of rare pet are you getting, Stone?" asked Roger.

Sonny mumbled something about his baby sister and brother.

"What kind?" taunted Roger.

Sonny looked unhappy. "I can't have a pet," he cried. "My mom and dad said they have enough work with the twins."

"And with you," sneered Roger.

Molly felt sorry for Sonny.

"You could get a real little pet," she whispered to him. "Or something that

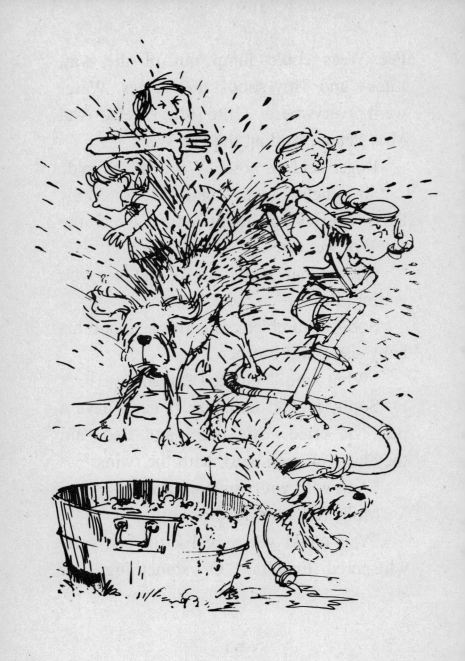

could live outside, like ants. That wouldn't bother your parents."

Sonny wiped his eyes. "I want a rare pet," he said.

"Ants would be rare," said Molly. "No one else has ants for a pet. You could get one of those ant farms and watch them work."

"I don't want ants," said Sonny. "But maybe they'd let me have a worm. A worm would be a rare pet, wouldn't it?"

Molly didn't like worms.

"It would be rare," she said. "But they are squirmy."

"That's okay," said Sonny. He dashed off to find his rare pet.

"My pet's going to be exotic," said Roger. "From another country."

"Maybe Roger is getting a monkey or something from a jungle," said Mary Beth to Molly on the way home.

Molly didn't care about Roger's pet. It would probably be something big and mean like he was. Something to get a lot of attention.

When Molly got home, a note in her mom's handwriting on the front door said, *Be back in a minute. Grocery store.* But on the steps, in a box with air holes, was a kitten. It was white with orange spots. There was a note in the box.

My name is Pumpkin, it said. *I have had my shots. Please give me a home.*

Molly could not believe her good luck. She cuddled the kitten in her arms. It purred softly. Molly put a little milk in a saucer and took the kitten and the milk up to her bedroom. Then she remembered that Mr. Sharp had said to put out water for your pets, so she put out another saucer with water in it. She put a doll blanket into the box for the kitten to sleep on. Then she called Mary Beth.

"My mom said someone called and asked for your address," Mary Beth said. "They needed a home for a kitten because they were moving out of town. They asked lots of questions about you."

"He's so cute," said Molly. "I wish he was mine to keep forever." She watched him sniff at the water.

"I'll tell everyone who calls to bring their homeless pets to you," said Mary Beth.

What a good friend! thought Molly.

"I'm bringing our dog and cat to the race," said Mary Beth. "But I don't think they'll win. They are too old."

Molly watched Pumpkin drink his water and jump back into the box. Then he went to sleep. Molly went downstairs to look for pictures of unusual animals for the scrapbook.

She had just found a magazine when

the front doorbell rang. Molly opened the door, and a little boy thrust a puppy into her arms.

"We've got too many," he said. "Our dog had puppies and we can't keep them all. Here is a bag of Pup Chow."

Molly couldn't believe her luck! She had just put the signs up and already had two temporary pets!

She took the puppy in and gave him some food. She set a dish of water in her room next to the cat box.

Before her parents came home, a man dropped off a bowl of twenty guppies, with their fish food. "We've got a million," said the man. "Take them."

Molly's room was getting crowded. She set the bowl of guppies on the floor. She put newspapers down for the puppy. Her mother would not like it if he wet on the floor or the rug.

While she was laying the newspapers, the kitten drank out of the fishbowl and scared the guppies. They swam around and around in their bowl frantically.

Molly sighed. The temporary pets were lots of work. I better put the guppies up high, she thought.

Molly set the fishbowl on her dresser and the kitten jumped right up beside it!

Molly carefully carried the bowl to the basement and put it on a table under a window, where the fish would get plenty of light.

The doorbell rang. Molly ran up the steps and saw a birdcage at the door. Inside was a small bird that talked. The woman who held it said, "If he talks too much, just put a cover over his cage. Then he will sleep."

Molly talked to the bird and thanked the lady. On the way to her room she remembered Sylvester and Tweetie Pie. A bird might not want to live in the same room as a cat.

Molly took the birdcage down to the basement and hung the cage from a hook on one of the rafters.

"There!" she said. "I'll come and visit you in the morning."

But the bird talked so much that Molly had to go down and cover his cage with her sweater. She found a carrot in the refrigerator and grated it. She put it between the bars of the cage.

At suppertime Mr. Duff said, "I think I hear a noise in the basement."

"No, you don't," said Molly quickly. "I mean, I don't hear anything."

"It's probably the furnace," said Mrs. Duff.

"Or the washing machine," said Molly. But she remembered, no one was washing.

The next morning Molly was up early. She took the puppy out in the backyard for a run. Then she fed him and brushed him.

She brushed the kitten and cleaned the box and got fresh water for the dishes.

"Squawk squawk!" said the bird when Molly took her sweater off his cage. She changed the paper in the bottom of the cage and gave him some birdseed the woman had brought along. She gave him water, and then shook some fish food into the guppy bowl. They were happy to see her. They all swam over toward her and toward the fish food.

"It's fun having pets that are glad to see me," she said to them. But the pets were a lot of work. "I'll have to do this every day until they are adopted!" she said.

At school that day she confided to

Mary Beth that she really didn't need any more pets.

"I think you should take those signs down," Mary Beth said. "My mom is getting tired of all the phone calls."

After school the girls took down the signs. Molly put up new ones in their place. FREE PETS TO GOOD HOMES, they said.

As Molly got close to home, a little girl handed her a box with air holes in it. Molly could hear scratching and chewing. Inside the box was a little brown mouse and a green frog.

"Oh, no!" cried Molly. "Where will I put them?"

Molly did not think a mouse would sleep well with a kitten in the room. Molly decided to put the mouse in the bathtub in a little box. And the frog could live in the laundry tub downstairs.

After playing with the animals and feeding them, Molly barely had time to do her homework. She fell into bed and went to sleep at once.

"Help," came a scream in the middle of the night. Molly jumped out of bed. She bumped into her father in the hall.

"Help!" came the scream again. Then her mother ran from the bathroom. "There is a MOUSE in there!" she cried.

"That's just Mickey," said Molly. "He's my temporary pet."

Her mother looked pale. "How long will he be staying?" asked Mrs. Duff.

"Just till I find him a home," said Molly. "I'll get my badge for finding him a home."

Molly's parents frowned. "Maybe he can live in the garage," said Mr. Duff. "I think I have an old hamster cage he'd like."

Mr. Duff took Mickey to the garage and they all went back to bed. The puppy snuggled up near Molly's chin. His cold nose touched her cheek. She wanted to keep him so badly!

The next morning Mrs. Duff said, "I went downstairs to put some clothes in the washer, and a green frog jumped out of the laundry tub at me."

"That's Homer," said Molly. "He's my temporary pet."

"I thought that Mickey was the temporary pet!" said her mother.

"They both are," said Molly, seeing that she could not fool her mother into thinking she had just one temporary pet. After all, anyone could tell the difference between a mouse and a frog.

Molly put water into the bathtub and gave Homer a swim. If none of them took a bath for a while, Homer could have his own private pool.

But at school the next day, Molly said to Mary Beth, "I may have to drop out of school to take care of my pets."

"Maybe some of the Pee Wees can adopt their pets from you instead of the pound," said Mary Beth. "Then they would be helping a pet, and so would you!"

But on Tuesday, the day of the Pee Wee pet race, Molly found the Pee Wees already had pets. And they were not adopted from Molly's home for homeless pets.

CHAPTER

A Squirmy Winner

"**W**hich pet are you bringing for the race?" asked Mary Beth before they left.

"My frog," said Molly. "He is my fastest temporary animal."

When the Pee Wees got to the meeting, they had all kinds of pets with them.

The Bakers brought their dog.

Lisa brought her bird in a cage.

Kevin had a hamster.

Sonny had a big worm in a shoe box filled with soil.

Tim had a grasshopper.

"Let's see your pet, Roger. Where is your rare exotic pet?" asked Rachel.

Roger reached under the table. He took out a fishbowl.

Everyone began to roar with laughter.

"A goldfish!" shrieked Tim.

"You said you were getting a jungle animal!" cried Sonny.

"This is no ordinary fish!" said Roger. "This fish is a Siamese fighting fish!"

The Pee Wees gathered around Roger. He held up the glass bowl that looked something like a drinking glass. It had a glass stem.

"This fish is from the Far East," said Roger. "This is no ordinary goldfish or guppy."

Molly had to admit this was not a goldfish. For one thing, it was not orange. It was dark blue and red. It had a big fan-like tail that changed color when it swished around the bowl.

"It's pretty," admitted Sonny. "But it's just a fish. It's no tiger."

"His dad wouldn't let him get a tiger," said Kenny. "Or even a big dog. Their apartment building says NO PETS."

Roger turned red.

"Well, where's your leopard, Stone?" he said, turning to Sonny.

Now Sonny had to admit he couldn't have a leopard because of the twins.

"I'm not afraid to have a leopard," he said. "It's just the twins. They'd be too scared. He might eat them up. Anyway, I've got something just as rare."

Sonny dug his worm out of the box.

"Ick!" said Rachel, making a face.

"Yuck," said Tracy. "I hate worms."

"A worm's not rare, dummy," said Roger.

"It's a rare pet," said Sonny. "My mom said so. They don't even sell them in pet stores, they are so rare."

Everyone had to admit they did not sell worms in pet stores. Except for other pets to eat.

Mrs. Peters clapped her hands.

"I think we'll have our races outside," she said. "I'll draw some chalk lines on the sidewalk."

"I know one pet that won't win a race," said Roger, pointing at Sonny's worm.

"His name is Sport," said Sonny. "And he is fast."

"Ho ho ho," laughed Roger.

Sonny took Sport out of his box and put him on the grass that edged the sidewalk.

"Look how long he is. This is a great worm. The longest one in town," said Sonny.

Roger lifted his foot and placed his shoe right over Sport's body. He pretended to lower his foot and stamp on him.

"Don't you dare step on Sport," cried Sonny, grabbing his pet. "And you're scaring him!"

The two boys began to fight, and Sport squirmed deeper into the grass.

"Get him!" yelled Sonny as he wrestled with Roger.

No one wanted to touch Sport. Finally Mrs. Peters broke up the fight and Sonny rescued his worm and put him on his shoulder.

"Can we show what tricks our pets can do, Mrs. Peters?" asked Roger. "Charlie can swim underwater. That's more than that old worm can do."

"My worm can sit up!" shouted Sonny.

The Pee Wees all began to laugh at the

idea of a worm sitting up. But Sonny had him in his hand now, and lifted his front end with a stick.

"See?" he said. "I think I should get a badge for having a pet worm that can sit up."

"It's time to get on with the races," said Mrs. Peters.

"I want to race with the frog and the worm." Kenny laughed. "My dog will win in one second!"

"Homer is faster than your dog," said Molly. "Just wait and see."

"My fish can't race," admitted Roger. "But if he could, he'd win."

"Neither can my bird," said Lisa. "He would fly away. But he'd win if there was a singing contest."

"It doesn't seem fair to have a worm and grasshopper race with the other animals," said Mrs. Peters.

"Yes, it does!" shouted Sonny. "Sport can win!"

"My grasshopper is fast!" said Tim.

"Not as fast as a dog or cat!" Molly laughed. "This ought to be good," she added.

"Sonny is going to feel bad," said Mary Beth. "He hates to lose."

"Rat's knees," said Molly. "Why does Sonny think a worm can win? He should have listened to Mrs. Peters when she said it wasn't fair. Now Sonny's going to be crying all over the place again."

Molly felt sorry for Sonny. It wasn't his fault he was such a baby. It was his mother's. Why didn't he admit a worm is too slow to be in a race?

"I want to race Sport against the puppy and kitten and frog and grasshopper," insisted Sonny.

"There will be a red ribbon for this

race," Mrs. Peters said, laughing.

"My worm will be wearing it!" said Sonny.

The animals were lined up on the sidewalk.

"We'll make this a very short race," said Mrs. Peters. "Just one or two feet."

She made a mark about a foot from the starting line. The owners stood at the finish line and whistled and called and shouted, but they could not touch their pets.

"Keep your voice soft," said Mrs. Peters. "Coax them gently and praise them. Don't frighten them," she added.

"One, two, three, GO!" shouted their leader.

"Come on, Sport!" called Sonny.

Roger was rocking with laughter.

"Come on, Hopper!" called Tim.

But the grasshopper was rubbing his

rear legs together and making the noise grasshoppers make at night in the woods. He did not move.

"He can hop real far," said Tim. "Real fast." Tim hopped on the grass to show the Pee Wees.

"Well, he's not moving now, Noon," said Roger.

The dog did move. But it was the wrong way. He turned around and ran away from the race.

Rachel's borrowed kitten closed her eyes and cuddled into a round ball on the starting line and fell asleep!

Molly placed Homer on the line carefully, and he flew through the air. But he flew into Molly's lap instead of over the finish line!

Sonny's worm was inching along, slowly, slowly, slowly.

In the right direction.

It squirmed toward the finish line!

The Pee Wees stood with their mouths open.

The kitten watched the grasshopper.

The puppy played on the grass.

The grasshopper rubbed his legs together.

The frog sat in Molly's lap.

But Sport inched along so slowly, he barely moved.

It took ten minutes. But finally Sport crawled across the finish line!

"What did I tell you?" said Sonny. "Didn't I tell you Sport would win?"

"I can't believe it," said Molly. "Sonny really did win!"

The Pee Wees clapped and cheered. They whistled and pounded Sonny on the back.

Mrs. Peters was laughing so hard, she

almost forgot the red ribbon. Then she took it out and pinned it on Sonny's shirt.

"I'd put it on Sport, but he has no collar!" She laughed.

"If that doesn't beat everything," said Mary Beth. "Sonny thinks his worm is so smart. And the only reason he won was just dumb luck."

Mrs. Peters and Mrs. Stone served refreshments out in the yard at the picnic table. Then the Pee Wees sang their song and said their pledge. It had been a fun meeting. Molly was glad that Sonny didn't end up crying.

Molly didn't mind not winning. But when she thought about all of her homeless pets, she felt sad. Maybe Sonny didn't cry, but right now Molly surely felt like it.

CHAPTER 5

The Last
Temporary Pet

When Molly got home, she fed and cleaned her temporary pets. She played with them. She took her puppy for a walk on his leash. Then she held him in her lap and rubbed his ears. He stood up and gave her a lick on her cheek.

"I love you too!" said Molly, hugging him.

After their walk, Molly sneaked in the back door just before her mother came out to shake a rug. She told her mother she would clean her own room this week.

At supper her mother said, "I have heard strange noises in this house lately."

"Maybe it's haunted," said Molly nervously.

"It doesn't sound like ghosts," said her mother.

"What do ghosts sound like?" asked Mr. Duff, laughing.

Mrs. Duff frowned. "Ghosts would moan and groan," she said. "This is more of a chipping and chirping." She eyed Molly.

"Ghosts could chip and chirp," said Molly. "They might even purr and growl. There might be animal ghosts."

"Our house is too new to be haunted," said Molly's dad, taking some more round steak. "There could be a something trapped in the chimney. That happened to the Kellys. I'll have to check."

Molly bit her bottom lip. If her dad went prowling around the basement checking the chimney, he might find her homeless pets! Even though she'd hidden them behind the furnace where they'd be nice and warm. Still, they had said she could have temporary pets. Or pet.

Molly wondered if she should confess. Blurt out her problem. If she didn't find homes soon, she'd have to.

She called Mary Beth and told her this was an emergency.

"I think my aunt wants a kitten," Mary Beth said.

"Really?" said Molly. "Can she take it tonight?"

"I'll call her," said Mary Beth.

In a little while Mary Beth's aunt called Molly.

"Is it long hair or short hair?" she asked. "How old is it, and what color? Has it had its shots? Is it a male or female?"

Molly didn't know how old it was. Or what shots it had. Or if it was a boy or girl. The aunt sounded doubtful.

"If I get it from the pound, it will have records," she said.

"But you have to pay money at some pounds," said Molly. "And this would be a Pee Wee Scout good deed."

Then she remembered that Mary Beth's aunt did not have to do good deeds. "It would be charity," she said.

The aunt laughed and said she'd be over to see it in an hour.

"I'll bring it to Mary Beth's," said Molly quickly, and hung up the phone before the aunt could argue.

Molly tied one of her hair ribbons around the kitten's neck to make a good adoption-impression. Then she wrapped it in a little blanket, making sure it could breathe.

She found her old raincoat with the big pockets and put the kitten into a pocket.

Molly was glad they had eaten early. It was still light out.

"I'm going over to Mary Beth's for just a minute," called Molly to her parents.

"What about homework?" asked her father.

"I don't have any," she called.

"Molly?" called her mother. "Is it raining out?"

"I don't think so," said Molly.

"Then why are you wearing that old raincoat?"

"It might rain," said Molly. "It's cloudy out."

The kitten squirmed in her pocket. "Meow!" it said.

Her father began to say something, but by that time Molly was out the door and down the street.

Mary Beth's aunt was waiting.

"Oh, it's darling!" she said. "What a darling little itty-bitty pussycat!"

Mary Beth's aunt slipped a few dollar bills into Molly's hand. "For the Pee Wees," she said. "For charity."

Molly thanked her and said good-bye and dashed home. She had one less pet! No more meowing that her mother might hear! Now if only she could find some other homes this fast!

The next day after school Mary Beth said, "Frogs like water. So do guppies. You could put them in a pond and they would be with other animals in a natural habitat. And the mouse would like to live in the woods. I've seen lots of mice in the woods. They are outdoor animals."

The Pee Wees had learned all about animals' habitats in second grade.

Mary Beth was right! One less frog

was one less haunted croak for her mother to hear! And one less mouse to scare her!

Molly and Mary Beth took the frog and the guppies to the pond. They let them go.

"Look how happy they are!" said Mary Beth as the fish swam away. The frog hopped under a bush.

They let the mouse out in the woods. He looked happy, too, as he ran off to join his friends.

"Now I only have the bird," said Molly.

She didn't mention the puppy. She couldn't stand to think of having him go, even though she knew he'd have to. She felt very close to him. He slept on her bed at night. When he chewed her slippers, Molly bought a chew toy at the pet store.

"Let's go door to door and ask if peo-ple would like a free pet," said Mary Beth.

Up one street and down another went the girls.

Up and down.

Up and down.

But either people had a pet or did not want a pet.

"That makes sense," said Molly, sitting on someone's front steps. "If they wanted a pet, they would go to the pound or to a pet shop and get one."

Mary Beth sighed.

As they sat there, Rachel came by with Lisa.

"What are you doing over here?" asked Rachel.

Molly told her.

"My mom says people shouldn't take in stray animals," she said.

"Mine aren't stray," said Molly.

"Do you know their family history?" demanded Rachel.

Molly didn't know animals had family histories!

"No," she said.

"Then they are strays," said Rachel.

"I think you should help us instead of criticizing," said Mary Beth to Rachel.

"I did my good deed for Animals Week," said Rachel. She sat down on the steps next to Molly. "I took Shep for a walk."

"Pooh, that's just a tiny good deed," said Mary Beth.

"It's enough to get my badge," said Rachel.

Rachel was right, thought Molly. Why hadn't she, Molly, chosen something simple? Why did she have to do something so noble? Then she thought how happy the kitten was with Mary Beth's aunt. And she thought how happy Mary Beth's aunt was!

The frog and guppies were happy in the pond. The mouse was happy in the woods. Now if she could place the last two, she would not only get her badge but she would feel like she'd done something special for animals.

"Well, the nursing home where my grandma works did say they wanted a bird to cheer up the patients," said Rachel. "Does your bird have a cage?"

"Yes!" said Molly, jumping to her feet. "If he didn't, he'd have flown away a long time ago!"

"I better call and be sure," said Rachel.

The girls ran to Rachel's house and called.

Molly held her breath as Rachel talked.

"Is it healthy?" asked Rachel, holding her hand over the receiver.

Molly nodded. "He's pretty, too, and he talks," she said.

Rachel talked to her grandma some more.

"Okay," she said, and hung up.

"She wants him," said Rachel. "I can take him and give him to my grandma."

Molly couldn't believe her luck. She ran up to Rachel and did something she had never thought she'd do. She threw her arms around her neck and hugged her.

Rachel even hugged her back!

"Now you have to do the puppy yourself," she said, straightening her blouse and looking embarrassed.

Molly went home and got the cage and the bird and the bird food. She put the cover over the cage so the bird would not get a chill.

By the time Molly's mother got home, she'd only have one temporary pet left to place!

A Permanent Pet

After Rachel took the bird, Molly ran home and swept up birdseed. She made everything look like there had never been a bird in the house.

Then she ran to her room and fed the puppy. She gave him a big hug. He put his front paws on her shoulders. He gave her a kiss.

"I wish I could keep you!" she said.

The puppy cocked his head to one side as if he understood her.

Molly cleaned her room really well and then took the puppy out in the backyard to play.

She brushed his soft hair and threw a little ball for him to chase.

"You should have a name," she told him. "Even if you are only temporary."

Molly thought and thought about a good name. She remembered a puppy in her reader at school was called Skippy.

"That's a good name for you!" she said.

The puppy dropped his ball in Molly's lap. He put his head there too. He felt warm and soft, and she could feel his little heart beat.

When her mother came home, Molly dashed to her room with Skippy. But

Skippy wanted to play ball. He began to bark.

"Arf! Arf!"

"Hush," whispered Molly, with her fingers on her lips. But it was too late. Her mother had heard the barks.

"Who is this?" she asked. "This is not the temporary frog!" she said. "Or am I seeing things?"

Molly decided it was time to tell her mother the truth.

"I wanted to have a home for animals," she said. "To get my badge."

When her dad came home, she told them about the pets she'd taken in.

"We figured that out," said Mr. Duff.

So they had known all along!

"But I found homes for all of them," said Molly. "Except Skippy."

"Good for you," said her dad. "But the next time you decide to open a home for wayward pigeons," said Mr. Duff, "you'd better ask first."

"Daddy! I'm not opening a pigeon home!"

Mr. Duff winked. He liked to be funny.

"Animals could have a disease," Mr. Duff went on, "and need medical help. They need the right food. And lots of attention. They could be very scared and bite you. They could even be dangerous."

"Skippy wouldn't bite me," said Molly, hugging the puppy.

"Still," said her father, "it's best to let us know when you have ideas for earning a badge."

Molly agreed she'd let him know before she opened a home for anything else.

"Now I think we should take our left-over pet to the vet for a checkup and some shots," said Mr. Duff.

At the vet there were all kinds of pets

with their owners. A beagle was with a tall man who had droopy ears like his pet.

There was a small boy with freckles who was with his cocker spaniel that had freckles.

"Skippy Duff!" called the nurse.

Molly and her father went in. The veterinarian examined Skippy and said he was in good health. Then he gave him his shots.

"You have a fine pet there!" said the doctor.

"He isn't mine," said Molly. "But I wish he was."

When they got home, Molly took Skippy for a walk. His fur was golden in the sunlight. Molly didn't want to think about finding him a home. Her feet dragged as she turned toward home.

At supper Mrs. Duff said, "Now Skippy is all ready to be adopted."

"I'll ask around the office," said Mr. Duff. "Maybe someone there would like a dog."

"I'll ask at work too," said Molly's mother.

Molly hoped no one would want a pet, so Skippy could stay with her longer.

Every day she fed Skippy. Every day she raced home from school to play with him. And every day she took him for a walk on his red leash, and washed his dirty food bowl. She'd made sure he had fresh water always available.

On Tuesday she took Skippy to the Pee Wee Scout meeting. He played with Lucky and Tiny in Mrs. Peters's fenced yard.

The Scouts worked on the giant scrapbook of pets. All the pictures Molly brought were of dogs.

"You're supposed to find unusual animals," said Tracy. "Those aren't unusual."

"They are too," said Molly. "No two dogs look alike."

Rachel rolled her eyes. "They all do," she said. "He's just an ordinary puppy."

How could Rachel call Skippy ordinary? He wagged his little tail when Molly came home from school. He fetched his ball for her. He was learning to sit up and beg. He was softer and cleaner and shinier and smarter than any puppy Molly had ever met! He was far from ordinary!

After they said their good deeds, Mrs. Stone came up to Molly. "I think I have found a home for Skippy," she said. "My brother, Sonny's uncle Rick, has a hobby farm and could use a good dog."

"Yeah," said Sonny. "We get to take your old dog to our farm. He'll be just like my dog. I'll get to play with him when we go there, and feed him and run him. We might even change his name!"

Molly wanted to give Sonny a shove. She wanted to tell him to keep his hands off her dog. How could they change his name? Skippy knew his name! He came when he was called. If he got another name now, it would confuse him!

"I think I'll call him Sport," said Sonny, pulling Skippy onto his lap.

"It will be a nice pet for Sonny," said Mrs. Stone, patting her son's head. "Even though we can't have one at home with the babies."

"It's just what he needs," agreed Mrs. Peters. "Since he is still a little j-e-a-l-o-u-s," she spelled.

How could Mrs. Peters agree to let Sonny take her lovely puppy away? Mrs. Peters was a traitor!

"I'll give your mother a call," said Sonny's mother, "and we can take him off your hands tonight." She went to use Mrs. Peters's phone.

Sonny began to pull Skippy's tail.

Didn't his mother realize what a brat Sonny could be? She had thought having a brother and sister would help Sonny grow up, but it hadn't. Sonny was as much of a baby as ever. A mean, nasty baby! Rat's knees! Why had Molly ever felt sorry for him?

On the way home with Skippy, Molly thought about hiding her pet. She thought about running away to Africa with him. Tears ran down her face.

Still, she had known Skippy was temporary. That was the agreement she'd made with her family. She'd find a home for the pets. The whole idea of taking

them in was to find new homes for them. And now she had. Every one of the animals was adopted. It was what she'd wanted. The thing she had not counted on was love. Molly had no idea a person could love a little wiggly puppy so much.

"Aren't we lucky?" asked her mother that evening. "To find such a good home! A hobby farm! With room to run and play."

Molly nodded and tried to keep the tears back. She took Skippy to her room to say good-bye to him.

Sport! What an awful name for her dog. She hugged him and squeezed him and stroked his golden body. Never again would she ever take in animals. Never again would she let herself love anything this much. This was the hardest badge she'd ever earned. If she had taken a strange dog for one walk as Rachel did, this never would have happened.

Molly heard the Stones downstairs. She didn't want to see them. She said good-bye for the last time and put Skippy out in the hall and closed her door tightly.

She fell onto her bed and cried.

"She must be asleep," whispered her mother, looking in.

But Molly wasn't sleeping. She was crying into her pillow.

"Give me my dog!" she heard Sonny shout as they went downstairs.

The voices got quieter as they left.

At breakfast Molly could not eat.

"Mrs. Stone said you could see Skippy whenever you want," said Mrs. Duff kindly.

"We could even bring him home for a day now and then," said her father.

"I don't want to see him!" shouted Molly. "I don't want to see him ever again!" She got up, kicking over her chair, and ran out the door to school.

"I got Molly's dog," sang Sonny on the playground. "Hey, Sport's out chasing squirrels right now," he added.

Skippy would not chase squirrels. He was a good, kind puppy. Or had been until Sonny's mean uncle got him.

"You can come and play with my dog," said Mary Beth, putting her arm around Molly after school. But Molly shook her head. She would try to forget about her pet. She would be glad when they got their badges and moved on to something new besides pets.

At home that night Molly found Skippy's ball under her bed. She had forgotten to send it with him. Before bed, she stepped on a piece of Pup Chow. She threw it away. There were things all over that reminded her of Skippy.

Molly's mother came in to tuck her into bed.

"I miss him too," she said. "He was beginning to feel like part of the family."

She turned out Molly's light.

Molly tossed and turned and finally fell asleep and dreamed about Skippy. The dream was so real that she actually heard him bark! She woke up and sat up in bed. She still heard the bark! How could it be a dream if she was wide awake?

"Yip! Yip! Yip!" Molly got up and looked out the window. Then she went downstairs to the back door. Something was scratching the door!

Molly left the safety chain on and looked out.

"Mom! Dad! It's Skippy!" she called. She opened the door and gathered the puppy in her arms. His heart was beating fast.

"Why, he must have come back home

all the way from Sonny's uncle's!" said Mr. Duff.

"That was a long walk!" said Mrs. Duff.

Molly poured him a saucer of water. He lapped it up quickly. His little tail wagged and wagged and he licked his family.

"He doesn't like it out there," said Molly.

Mr. Duff looked thoughtful. He looked at Mrs. Duff.

"I think," he said, "since Skippy walked all that way home to find us, he must really want to live here. I say we keep him."

Molly couldn't believe her ears! Skippy was hers! Not Sonny's!

"I'll call Rick in the morning and see if it's okay," he said.

Molly crossed all her fingers for luck. She even crossed her legs and arms.

In the morning her dad called Sonny's uncle. His uncle said he could get another dog! A bigger one!

Skippy was really and truly hers! It was like a miracle.

On Tuesday Mrs. Peters said, "We have all worked very, very hard on our Be Kind to Animals good deed. But I think Molly has worked hardest of all."

All of the Pee Wees cheered. And clapped. Even Sonny.

"We have all helped pets, and we have all learned a lot about animals," Mrs. Peters went on. "And now I will pass out the badges."

The badge was nice. It had a puppy's and a kitten's face on it. With two brown ears sticking up, the dog looked just like Skippy!

"You should get two badges," said

Mary Beth after they had sung their song and said their pledge.

"I did get two," said Molly. "I got a badge and I got a pet. A permanent pet all my own."

Rat's knees, she thought. No one could ask for more than that!

We love our country

And our home,

Our school and neighbors too.

As Pee Wee Scouts,

We pledge our best

In everything we do.

Be a Pee Wee Scout!

In *Piles of Pets,* the Pee Wee Scouts hope to adopt some rare and unusual pets.

The rarest animals of all are called *endangered species.* These animals are in danger of becoming extinct. The dodo bird is just one example of an animal that has been lost to us forever. But not every endangered species goes extinct. Sometimes people can work together to *save* an endangered species!

The **California condor** is one scary bird. A big black vulture that eats dead animals, it has the largest wingspan of any bird in North America (about nine feet!).

They might look tough, but these birds came very close to extinction. In 1987, there were only twenty-two California condors in the entire world! Scientists captured all of them. They hoped that they could keep the birds safe. They also hoped that the birds would lay more eggs in a zoo than they would in the wild. And the zoo could protect those eggs from other animals.

The scientists were successful, though they had to get creative. At times, they had to raise a baby condor away from its parents, using condor puppets to feed the young bird! They also taught the condors to stay away from power lines, so that the birds would be safer when they left the zoo.

Today there are over 300 California condors. About half of them live in the wild. They're still endangered, but they've made an impressive recovery. And luckily, they're not as scary as they look.

The **koala** looks like a living, breathing teddy bear. Just over a century ago, millions of the furry animals lived in Australia. Then, in the early twentieth century, people hunted them for their fur until they were nearly extinct.

The Australian government came to the koala's rescue with strict laws to protect it from hunters. Those laws are still in place today. It's also illegal to keep a koala as a pet.

No one knows for sure how many koalas live in the wild now. But the koala is definitely not in as much danger as it was 100 years ago. In fact, so many koalas live on Australia's Kangaroo Island that they are considered pests!

* * *

The **sea otter** is another animal that was hunted for its fur. In fact, otter fur was once so valuable that otters' pelts were nicknamed "soft gold." Hunters wanted more and more pelts, and the animals became rarer and rarer.

Finally, in 1911, people realized that otter hunting was a major problem for the whole world. The United States and several other countries signed the Treaty for the Preservation and Protection of Fur Seals. The treaty made it illegal to hunt

sea otters. As a result, there are many more otters living in the wild today than there were 100 years ago.

However, the sea otter is still endangered. Some people hunt the otters even though it's illegal. Illegal hunting is called *poaching*.

Fishing nets also mean trouble for sea otters. Since otters are mammals, they must breathe air. If they get stuck in an underwater net, they can drown.

But oil spills are by far the greatest danger to sea otters. When its fur is coated with oil, an otter is no longer protected from the cold. And breathing oil fumes is very bad for an otter's health.

The good news is that many people work to protect these animals. Some create safer fishing equipment. Others arrest poachers or refuse to buy anything a poacher sells. And many people work to prevent oil spills. But just in case there *is* a spill in the future, teams of scientists are trained and ready to come to the sea otter's rescue!

The **American alligator** is a survivor. Even when the dinosaurs died out 65 million years ago, this species lived on. But in the twentieth century, the alligator faced a threat the dinosaurs never did: human beings.

Alligators used to thrive in the huge Florida swamps called the Everglades. Then, in the 1940s and 1950s, new technology made it possible to change some of the swamps into farmland. Humans moved in and built towns, and the alligators lost much of their habitat. At the same time, people hunted alligators for their skins.

Fortunately, people realized what they were doing before it was too late. The alligator was named an endangered species. It became illegal to hunt them. Alligator farms were created to protect the animals and their eggs, and to educate the public.

By 1987, the alligator was no longer listed as an endangered species. Thanks to human teamwork, it looks like the American alligator might just be around for the next 65 million years.

The **Palos Verdes blue** is probably the rarest butterfly in the world. It lives only on the Palos Verdes Peninsula, outside Los Angeles, California.

In fact, this insect is so rare that it was once believed to be extinct! In 1983, construction on the peninsula caused many of

the butterflies to die. Scientists feared that none were left.

But they were in for a surprise. In 1994, a group of Palos Verdes blue butter-flies was found—on the *other* side of the peninsula!

Scientists took the butterfly off the list of *extinct* animals—but they put it on the

list of *endangered* species right away. That's because the problems the butterflies faced back in 1983 are still problems today. The butterfly can only lay its eggs on a plant called common deerweed. And as people in California build more homes, common deerweed is becoming *uncommon*. That means fewer butterfly eggs.

Scientists have set up tents where they

can grow deerweed and protect caterpillars until they become butterflies. It's a lot of work, but everyone's happy that the Palos Verdes blue has a second chance.

What can YOU do?

The best thing anyone can do for an endangered species is to cut down on pollution. Changes in the environment threaten every animal, from the pets in our backyards to the creatures of the rain forests and polar ice caps. Take as many steps as you can to reduce, reuse, and recycle . . . and you'll be a true friend to animals far and wide.

About the Author

Judy Delton was born and raised in St. Paul, Minnesota. She was the author of more than 200 books for children. She was also successful as a teacher, a speaker, and a class clown. Raising a family  of four children, she used the same mix of humor and seriousness that she considered important parts of any good story. She died in St. Paul in 2001.

About the Illustrator

Alan Tiegreen has illustrated many books for children, including all the Pee Wee Scouts books. He and his wife currently live in Atlanta, Georgia.